Dirty Bertie

LOO!

To Chris Newton and Heather Collins of the
Scottish Book Trust - thank you for looking
after me so well ~ D R
For Megan and Bethany with love ~ A M

STRIPES PUBLISHING
An imprint of Magi Publications
1 The Coda Centre, 189 Munster Road,
London SW6 6AW

A paperback original
First published in Great Britain in 2010

Characters created by David Roberts
Text copyright © Alan MacDonald, 2010
Illustrations copyright © David Roberts, 2010

ISBN: 978-1-84715-114-8

Printed and bound in the UK

10 9 8 7 6 5 4 3 2 1

Dirty Bertie
LOO!

DAVID ROBERTS WRITTEN BY **ALAN MACDONALD**

Collect all the
Dirty Bertie books!

Contents

LOO!

CHAPTER 1

"NO RUNNING!" barked Miss Boot, grabbing Bertie's arm as he flew past. "And that means you, Bertie. Get on the coach in an orderly fashion."

The class stampeded up the steps as Mr Weakly counted them on board. Bertie, Darren and Eugene elbowed their way past, trying to reach the back seat.

Dirty Bertie

Bertie raced down the aisle and skidded to a halt. Know-All Nick, and his weedy pal Trevor, had got there first.

"Sorry, Bertie," smirked Nick. "No room!"

"Yeah, no room!" grinned Trevor.

"But *we're* sitting there!" said Bertie.

Mr Weakly came down the gangway, looking flustered. He was a nervous young teacher who Bertie had once locked in the store cupboard for a dare.

"Come on, boys," he sighed. "Sit down. We're waiting to go."

"But sir, they're in our seats!" complained Bertie.

"Yeah, they had the back seat on the way here," said Darren.

"Tough cheese! First come, first served," said Nick, smugly.

Dirty Bertie

"Couldn't you all just share nicely?"
pleaded Mr Weakly. He could see Miss
Boot glaring at them like a black cloud.

Dirty Bertie

Bertie pointed at the empty seat in front. "Oh, Nick, isn't that your money?"

"Where?"

"There – under the seat!"

Nick got up to look. "Where…?"

WHOOSH!

Bertie and his friends barged past him and hurled themselves on to the back seat, pushing Trevor out of the way.

"Sorry! First come first served!" grinned Bertie.

"Sir!" whined Nick. "They stole our seats! It's not fair!"

"NICHOLAS!" Miss Boot's voice shook the windows like a hurricane. "SIT DOWN, THIS MINUTE!"

Nick flopped sulkily into the seat in front. The coach set off.

Bertie stared out of the window.

Dirty Bertie

The day had been one big let down. School trips were meant to be fun, but Miss Boot always chose something "educational". Why couldn't they go somewhere interesting – like a chocolate factory, or a space centre? Miss Boot's idea of a trip was to drag them hundreds of miles to the Costume Museum in Dribbleswick. Bertie had spent hours staring at dummies dressed in petticoats and frilly bloomers. Worse still, the museum shop didn't even sell sweets. He'd ended up buying a useless plastic ruler that said "I'VE BEEN TO THE COSTUME MUSEUM!" Bertie took it out of his bag and stared at it. Hang on, maybe he could find a use for it after all?

Dirty Bertie

The back of Nick's head was poking up above the seat in front. Bertie reached out and prodded it with his ruler. Nick scratched his head.

PROD! PROD! Bertie did it again. Nick swung round.

"Was that you?"

"What?" said Bertie, innocently.

"I'll tell," warned Nick, turning back. Bertie bent back the ruler, taking aim.

Dirty Bertie

THWUCK!

"OWW!" howled Nick, clutching his head. "Miss! Bertie hit me!"

Miss Boot spun round. "BERTIE! IS THIS TRUE?"

"No, Miss," said Bertie. After all, he hadn't touched Nick, the ruler had.

Nick narrowed his eyes. There was a long journey ahead. He would get Bertie for this.

CHAPTER 2

The coach crawled along slowly, nosing through traffic. Bertie felt like they'd been on it for a week. He had drunk the last of his lemonade while Eugene and Darren drew pictures of Miss Boot on the window. At long last they pulled off the motorway into a service station.

"We're stopping for fifteen minutes!"

boomed Miss Boot. "You will stay with me and Mr Weakly. And you will *all* be going to the toilet!"

The class filed into the service station with Miss Boot leading the way. They divided into two groups, with Mr Weakly taking the boys off to the men's toilets. But when they arrived there was a large notice outside:

CLOSED FOR CLEANING

"Oh dear! How unfortunate!" groaned Mr Weakly. "We'll try the café. Follow me, boys."

Bertie had had enough of staying with Mr Weakly. Besides, he didn't even need the loo. And he had spotted arcade games in the foyer.

"Hey, look," he whispered to Darren

and Eugene. "Let's stay here!"

"No!" said Eugene. "I need the loo!"

"Me too," said Darren.

"Fine," said Bertie. He hung behind as the others trooped into the café.

Ten minutes later, he'd shot down fifteen Vargon spaceships and reached level nine. But he'd started to squirm in his seat. Maybe he did need the toilet after all? Luckily, he still had a few minutes. He rushed to the café…

Nooo! The queue for the toilet stretched for miles.

Bertie looked for Darren and Eugene but they'd been and gone. He spotted Know-All Nick near the front of the queue. Normally he wouldn't have dreamed of asking Nick for anything, but this was an emergency.

"Hey, Nick," said Bertie. "Let me in. I really need the loo."

"There's a queue," said Nick.

"I know," replied Bertie. "But I can't wait. And the coach'll be going any minute. Please!"

Nick raised his eyebrows. "Ahh, poor Bertie. Are you really bursting?"

"Yes!"

"Would you like to go in front of me?"

"Can I?"

"No chance," snapped Nick. "Get to the back."

Bertie drooped to the end of the queue. Through the café window he could see Mr Weakly counting children on to the coach. The queue inched forward at a snail's pace. Nick came out of the toilet and hurried past.

Dirty Bertie

"Don't wet your pants, Bertie!" he jeered.

Finally Bertie reached the front.

KERSPLOOSH! The toilet flushed. *Yes! My turn at last!*

But just as the toilet door opened, someone grabbed him by the arm and hauled him out of the café.

"BERTIE! Come *on!*" fumed Miss Boot. "EVERYONE IS WAITING!"

"But Miss, I need—"

"We are late! Back on the coach. NOW!"

Bertie's classmates cheered as Miss Boot frogmarched him up the steps. The driver started the engine and the coach pulled away.

Darren turned to Bertie. "You all right? You look a bit pale."

"I NEED THE LOOOOOOO!" wailed Bertie.

CHAPTER 3

Cars and lorries zoomed past. Bertie tried to count them to keep his mind off other things.

"Thirty, thirty-one, thirty-loo…"

It was no good, all he could think about was needing the toilet. How long would it be until they got back to school? He wasn't sure he could hold out much longer. His tummy ached. His hands were sweating. Why oh why hadn't he gone when he had the chance?

He nudged Darren.

"Darren, I need the loo!"

"I know, you already told me."

"But I REALLY need it. Like, now."

"You can't go now! There's no toilet on the coach!" said Darren.

"I know that!" groaned Bertie.

"So what are you going to do?"

"That's what I'm asking you!"

Eugene leaned over. "What's up?"

"Bertie needs a wee," replied Darren.

"What? A piddle?"

"A widdle."

"A tiddle?"

"SHUT UP!" groaned Bertie. "You're not helping!"

Dirty Bertie

Darren and Eugene grinned. They were starting to enjoy this.

"D'you know what I do when *I* need to go?" said Darren. "I sing to myself."

Bertie sighed. "Don't be stupid."

"No, really! It works, doesn't it, Eugene?"

"Yeah," said Eugene. "It takes your mind off it. Go on, Bertie."

Bertie rolled his eyes. Still, he'd try anything if it stopped him thinking about what he was trying not to think about.

"All right. What shall I sing?" he asked.

Dirty Bertie

"I know," said Darren. He whispered something to Eugene. They burst into song:

"Does the driver want a wee wee?

Does the driver want a wee wee?

Does the driver—"

"SILENCE!" thundered Miss Boot, jumping to her feet. "WHO WAS THAT?"

Know-All Nick raised his hand. "Bertie, Miss."

"It wasn't ME!" cried Bertie. "Honest."

Miss Boot glowered. "I have my eye on you, Bertie. Do not try my patience." She sat back down.

Darren and Eugene fell about giggling. Bertie scowled at them.

"How'd you like it if you were dying for the loo and all I did was make jokes?" he grumbled.

Darren shrugged. "If it's that bad, tell Miss Boot," he said.

"How's that going to help?"

"You never know, maybe she'll stop the coach."

Bertie doubted it. Miss Boot didn't like to be bothered on coach trips. She especially didn't like to be bothered by him. Nevertheless, he had to try.

He got up and began to make his way down the gangway.

"Where are you going?" asked Know-All Nick.

"Mind your own business," said Bertie.

He found Miss Boot marking a pile of books with a red pen.

Bertie coughed loudly. "'Scuse me, Miss, I, um ... need the toilet."

Miss Boot looked up. "WHAT?"

"I need the toilet," said Bertie. "Badly."

Miss Boot snorted. "Go and sit down."

"But Miss, I can't wait..."

"Then why didn't you go at the service station like everyone else?" snapped Miss Boot. She stared accusingly at Mr Weakly.

"Oh dear!" he said meekly. "I thought they all did."

"I didn't have time!" moaned Bertie. "I was about to go when you made me get on the coach!"

Dirty Bertie

Miss Boot sighed wearily. "Why is it always you, Bertie?"

Bertie didn't answer. He was hopping from one foot to the other like a morris dancer.

Miss Boot slammed her book shut. "Well, there's nothing I can do now. We're on the motorway. You'll just have to wait till we get back to school."

Bertie moaned. "How long will that be?"

Miss Boot looked at her watch. "About an hour."

CHAPTER 4

Bertie drummed his feet on the floor. He stood up, then sat back down. He squirmed. He wriggled. He bounced up and down in his seat.

"Do you have to?" sighed Darren.

"I can't help it! I need to goooo!" wailed Bertie.

This was torture. Agony. And the rain

wasn't helping. Large raindrops ran down
the window. Drip, drip, drip. He felt like
he was going to explode. It was no
good. He would never last out. He stood
up and began to shuffle down the
gangway. Know-All Nick stuck
out an arm to bar
his way.

"Why can't you
sit still?" he asked.

"What's it to
you?" said Bertie.

"I know!" said
Nick, smiling.
"YOU need the toilet!"

"No I don't!" said Bertie, turning pink.

"Yes you do! BERTIE NEEDS THE
LOO-HOO!" sang Nick at the top of
his voice.

Dirty Bertie

People were turning round. Bertie pushed past and hurried towards Miss Boot.

"Um, Miss?"

Miss Boot let out a long sigh. "You again? What now?"

"I still need the toilet. Desperately!"

"I told you before, you'll have to wait."

"I caaaaan't!" moaned Bertie, crossing his legs. "Can't we stop, just for a minute?"

"We're on the motorway!" barked Miss Boot. "Where do you suggest we stop?"

Dirty Bertie

"At a service station!"

"There isn't another one. And stopping on the motorway is against the law. You'll just have to hold out."

Bertie whimpered. "I don't think I can!"

"You will."

"But what if I can't?"

Miss Boot groaned. "I don't know, go in a bottle!"

Bertie returned to his seat with the look of someone who was doomed. Still, Miss Boot had said it, and when a teacher told you to do something he assumed they meant what they said. And what else could he do? He rummaged in his backpack and found his empty lemonade bottle. He unscrewed the lid, checked that no one was watching and slid into the corner.

Dirty Bertie

Then Bertie did it. The thing that
would have made his parents blush with
shame and his classmates
howl in horror.
A smile of huge
relief spread
across his face.

Darren looked
over. "Ewww! You
haven't?"

"What?" asked Eugene.

"Bertie's weed in a bottle!"

"YOU DIDN'T!"

"All right, keep your voice down," said
Bertie. "Nobody saw, did they? Anyway,
Miss Boot told me to."

He carefully screwed the lid back on.

Eugene pulled a face. "Yuck! What are
you going to do with it?"

Dirty Bertie

Bertie hadn't thought that far ahead. He couldn't sit there holding a full bottle of wee. Somebody might notice! He unzipped the pocket of his backpack and stuffed the bottle inside. He could dump it somewhere on the way home.

At four o'clock the coach pulled up outside the gates. Bertie had never been so happy to be back at school. He put on his backpack and joined the queue to get off. Know-All Nick jostled him from behind.

Dirty Bertie

"Get a move on, slowcoach! I thought you needed the loo!"

"There's a queue, fat face," said Bertie.

He jumped down the steps and waited for Darren and Eugene on the pavement. Just as they were going a reedy voice behind them cried out, "Oh, Bertie! Look what I've got!"

Bertie turned round.

Know-All Nick was waving a plastic bottle. It wasn't! It couldn't be! Bertie checked the pocket of his backpack. ARGHHH! It had gone!

"I've got your drink, Bertie! Na na nee na naa!" jeered Nick.

"Crumbs!" gasped Eugene. "D'you think we ought to tell him?"

Bertie thought about it. "No, why spoil it? He'll soon find out if he gets thirsty!"

DIG!

CHAPTER 1

"Mum, can I have an ice cream?" asked Bertie.

"No, you've just had lunch!"

"But I'm still hungry!"

"You're not hungry, you're just greedy. Now find something to do."

Bertie flopped down on the sand. They had been at Slopton-on-Sea for almost a

Dirty Bertie

week and he had done everything there was to do. It was okay for his parents — they *liked* doing nothing. And Suzy could lie around doing nothing for hours. But Bertie wanted to play. He stared at the windswept beach and the grey sky. If only Darren or Eugene were here — then they could play football, or pirates … or maybe pirate football.

Suddenly Mum got to her feet. "Goodness, isn't that the Riches over there?"

Dirty Bertie

Bertie turned to look. A couple were coming their way loaded down with rugs, bags and beach chairs. Trailing behind was a goofy boy with lank, fair hair. Bertie groaned. *Not Royston Rich! What's HE doing here?* Royston was in Bertie's class and Bertie couldn't stand him. He was the biggest boaster in the school. Whatever anyone had, Royston had one that was bigger, better and ten times more expensive.

Dirty Bertie

"Good heavens!" cried Mrs Rich, raising her sunglasses. "Fancy seeing you!"

"Yes," said Mum. "I didn't know you came here on holiday."

"It's our first time," said Mrs Rich. "Gerald's sister has a house by the beach, doesn't she, Gerald?"

"Actually it's more of a villa," yawned Gerald. "What about you?"

"Oh, we've just rented a little flat," said Mum.

"Actually it's more of an apartment," said Dad quickly.

"And here's Bertie!" squawked Mrs Rich. "Isn't that super, Royston? You'll have a little playmate!"

"Super," said Royston, glaring at Bertie.

"Lovely," said Mum. "Bertie's been moaning that he's missing his friends.

Dirty Bertie

Why don't you two run along and play?"

Bertie groaned. Play with Royston?
He'd rather wrestle an octopus!

"So," sighed Royston, "what shall we do?
Want to see my new remote control
plane?"

"No thanks," said Bertie. "I'm busy."

He picked up his spade and
began digging the hole he'd
started earlier.

"That's rubbish!" sniffed
Royston. "Why don't
you make it
bigger?"

"I *am* making
it bigger,"
scowled Bertie.

Dirty Bertie

"Your spade's too small. Why don't you get a better one?"

Bertie went on shovelling sand. He would have liked to bury Royston up to his neck.

"I'm getting a new bucket and spade for the competition," boasted Royston.

Bertie stopped digging. "What competition?"

"The sandcastle competition, stupid. Didn't you know? There's a prize and everything."

Bertie's eyes lit up. A sandcastle competition? With a prize? Why hadn't anyone told him? In Bertie's opinion, he was brilliant at building sandcastles.

"When is this competition?" he asked.

"Tomorrow," said Royston. "Maybe you should enter so you can watch me win.

Dirty Bertie

I already know what I'm going to make
and it'll be *miles* better than yours."

"Want to bet?" said Bertie.

"Suits me." They shook hands.

"See you tomorrow then!" said
Royston, swaggering off with his nose in
the air.

Bertie watched him go. He would
teach that goofy-faced show-off how to
make a sandcastle. Wait till tomorrow,
then they'd see who was best!

CHAPTER 2

That evening, Bertie's family ate supper back at the flat. Whiffer hovered beside Bertie's chair hoping he would drop some chips on the carpet.

"Dad," said Bertie. "Can I enter a sandcastle competition? They're having one on the beach tomorrow. Royston reckons he's going to win."

44

"Huh! I bet he does!" said Dad. "We'll see about that."

"His dad's buying him a new bucket and spade," said Bertie.

"Typical," said Dad. "We'll get you a new one in the morning."

"That's not fair!" grumbled Suzy. "What about me?"

Mum rolled her eyes. "Aren't you taking this a bit seriously? It's only a sandcastle competition! It's meant to be fun. What does it matter who wins?"

"Of course it matters!" said Dad. "I'm not letting Gerald Rich's son win."

"Why not?"

"Because he's a smelly-pants show-off!" answered Bertie.

"Exactly," said Dad. "Anyway, we're bound to win. We just need to think of something clever."

"WE?" said Bertie.

"Yes, me and you. We can be a team."

Bertie's mouth fell open. "But it's a children's competition!"

"Don't worry," said Dad. "I'm not going to interfere, I'll just be there to offer advice."

Bertie had heard this before. When his dad offered advice it usually ended with him taking over completely. Like the time he'd helped with Bertie's history project and had stayed up half the night making an Egyptian pyramid out of yoghurt pots. Bertie didn't want to be the only boy in the competition who'd brought along his Dad. It would be so embarrassing!

Dad stroked his chin. "The question is what to make? It's got to be something

eye-catching. What about the Houses of
Parliament?"

"No!" groaned Bertie.

"Or the Eiffel Tower?"

"No!"

"Or an airport with planes and
runways and a control tower…"

"NO, NO!" cried Bertie. "Dad, I'd
rather do it by myself. Please."

Dirty Bertie

Mum patted Dad on the arm. "Maybe Bertie's right. You come shopping with me and Suzy."

"Okay!" sighed Dad. "I'm only trying to help you win."

"It's not the winning that counts," said Mum. "It's the taking part."

Bertie said nothing. Anyone could take part. He wanted to *win*. But if he was going to beat Royston he needed a good idea. Everyone would be making crummy old sandcastles; his entry had to be something different. Something no one else would think of. He glanced down. Whiffer was still eyeing his chips with his tongue hanging out. That was it! Of course! Instead of a sand-castle he'd make a *sand-dog*! It was different, it was original and best of all he could get

Dirty Bertie

Whiffer to act as his model. Bertie
sneaked a chip off his plate and dropped
it on the carpet. That prize was as good
as his!

CHAPTER 3

Next morning Bertie arrived at the
beach with his brand-new bucket and
spade. Whiffer trotted eagerly at his
heels. It was a bright, breezy day, with a
few grey clouds out to sea. A large
crowd of children had turned up for
the competition. Bertie noticed many
of them had brought shells and flags

and other stuff to decorate their
sandcastles.

"You're sure you don't want us to
stay?" asked Dad.

"No, it's okay," said Bertie. "Whiffer will
keep me company."

"Can we go to the shops now?"
moaned Suzy.

Mum glanced at the sky. "It looks a bit
cloudy," she said. "You better take my
umbrella just in case. We'll be back for
the judging. Good luck, Bertie," she
called, as they headed off.

Royston Rich pushed his way through
the crowd. Like Bertie he had a brand-
new bucket and spade, though his were
big enough to dig to Australia.

"Hello, Bertie! Come to watch me
win?" he smirked.

"In your dreams," said Bertie.

Just then Mr Rich appeared. Bertie stared. He was carrying a new bucket and spade too.

"Wait," said Bertie. "Your dad's not entering – is he?"

"Oh yes, didn't I mention it?" said Royston. "Parents are allowed to help – it's in the rules. Luckily my dad's *brilliant* at making sandcastles."

Dirty Bertie

Bertie glanced around. It seemed everyone else was here with their mum, dad or grandma. He was the only one entering by himself! He looked for his dad, but it was too late – he'd already gone. That two-faced rat Royston. He'd done this on purpose!

A large square of sand had been roped off for the competition. A woman wearing huge baggy shorts stood on a box to address everyone. She had a whistle round her neck and a clipboard in her hand. Bertie thought she looked like Miss Boot's ugly sister.

"You have one hour to complete your sandcastles," she barked. "When time is up I shall blow one blast on my whistle, like so. PEEEEP! That means put down your buckets and spades, immediately. I will come round with the other judges to inspect your work. Any questions? Splendid. Then on my whistle, begin!"

PEEEEP!

Everyone began digging furiously. Parents drew lines in the sand while their children stood by looking baffled. Royston and his dad were digging like slaves and had already produced a mountain of sand. Bertie, meanwhile, was trying to get Whiffer to pose.

"Sit boy! Sit!" he ordered. But Whiffer was too excited to sit. There was nothing he liked better than digging.

"SIT!" yelled Bertie.

He wrestled Whiffer's bottom to the ground and began to dig. Whiffer barked joyfully and bounded over to help. He kicked up showers of sand in all directions. Bertie sighed. So much for using Whiffer as a model! He'd just have to work from memory.

He set to work as Whiffer ran back and forth, leaving a trail of paw prints over a dozen sandcastles. Bertie pretended it wasn't his dog.

Dirty Bertie

Forty minutes later, he stopped to wipe the sweat from his face. Building sandcastles was hard work. The grey clouds had drifted closer. The woman in baggy shorts passed by.

"Ah!" she said. "That is … hmm … well, what is it?"

"It's my dog," said Bertie. She was obviously blind as a bat.

"Really? Good heavens! Is there something wrong with him?"

"No," said Bertie, glancing round for Whiffer. He caught sight of him halfway up the beach chasing a flock of seagulls.

"Never mind, keep at it!" barked Baggy Shorts. "You've only got five more minutes."

Dirty Bertie

She marched off, checking her watch and glancing at the dark sky.

Bertie took a step back to inspect his work. Even he had to admit it hadn't turned out quite as well as he'd hoped. His sand-dog looked more like a melting snowman. One lumpy blob stood on top of a bigger lumpy blob. The top one could have been a head but it was hard to tell. The nose was squashed, one eye had fallen off and the paws stuck out like a pair of mud pies.

Dirty Bertie

Bertie turned to check out the competition. He stared boggle-eyed. Some of the other entries were amazing! There were playful dolphins, tiny sea horses and fairy castles covered with pink shells. Next to him was a

Dirty Bertie

mermaid with seaweed hair. And best
of all was a speedboat so real that it
seemed to be skimming the waves. At
the wheel was a goofy boy in a sailor's
cap. Royston Rich. He caught sight of
Bertie and waved.

Dirty Bertie

Bertie's shoulders drooped. There was no way he was going to win. Royston's speedboat would walk it. And for the next million years he'd have to endure his endless boasting at school.

By now a crowd of people had gathered to watch. Bertie spotted his parents among them. They had rescued Whiffer, and Suzy was trying hard to stop him running off again.

Big black clouds blotted out the sun as Baggy Shorts climbed on to her box and blew a blast on her whistle. PEEEEP!

"Time's up!" she barked. "Everyone put down your—"

But her words were drowned out, as the clouds burst and the rain came pouring down.

CHAPTER 4

Everyone fled. Children dropped their spades and ran. Bertie's family ran too, finding shelter under the roof of the Beach Café.

"Where's Bertie?" asked Mum, suddenly.

Dad stared. "I thought he was with us!"

Dirty Bertie

Suzy shrugged her shoulders. "Don't ask me, I was holding Whiffer but he ran off."

They peered through the pouring rain. The beach was empty apart from one large yellow umbrella. Under it they could just make out a boy and a dog sitting next to a shapeless lump of sand.

Dirty Bertie

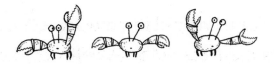

At last the rain stopped and everyone crept back to see what was left of the sandcastles.

The beach looked like a battlefield. The mermaid was a clump of seaweed, while Royston's speedboat was a soggy heap. Everywhere lay messy blobs of sand which had once been dolphins or sea horses.

The judges huddled together for a moment and Baggy Shorts climbed back on to her box.

"I regret to say the competition has been cancelled," she said. "The rain has ruined everything. There's really nothing left we can judge."

"Yes there is!" Everyone turned round. It was the boy with the dog.

"Look," shouted Bertie. "It's all right! I kept it dry!"

The judges stared. Bertie's sandcastle resembled an alien from the planet Blob. Nevertheless, it was the only entry left. They mumbled together, and finally Baggy Shorts turned to face the crowd.

"I'm pleased to announce that we have a winner. First prize goes to, um…"

Bertie whispered in her ear.

"To Bertie for his … er … unusual portrait of a dog. Well done!"

Dirty Bertie

Bertie stepped forward to receive his prize. It was a giant hamper stuffed with cakes, sweets, toffee apples and goodies. As he carried it off he passed a goofy, red-faced boy throwing a tantrum. Bertie gave Royston a cheery wave.

Victory had never tasted so sweet!

CHAPTER 1

Bertie was watching TV when Mum and Dad burst into the lounge.

"Great news!" beamed Dad, excitedly.

"We're getting a hamster!" cried Bertie.

"No, better than that, we're moving house!"

Bertie almost fell off the sofa.

"MOVING?" he gasped. "When?"

"As soon as we've sold our house," said Dad. "It's going up for sale next week. Isn't that marvellous?"

"But I don't want to move," said Bertie.

"Where would we live?" asked Suzy.

"In Poshley Green," said Mum. "It's a much nicer area and we've already seen a house we like!"

"But I don't want to move!" grumbled Bertie, raising his voice.

Mum took no notice. "It's got a lovely long garden and a park over the road. And wait till you see the size of your bedroom, Suzy."

"Cool!" said Suzy.

"BUT I DON'T WANT TO MOVE!" yelled Bertie, jumping up and down.

Mum sighed. Dad frowned. "How do you know?" he said. "You haven't even seen the house yet."

"I like *our* house," said Bertie. "It's got my bedroom and all my stuff."

"Well you can take your stuff with you," replied Dad.

"And I'm sure you'll make lots of new friends," said Mum.

"What for?" asked Bertie. "I've got friends already."

"I mean at your new school."

New school? Bertie stared. Had they all gone raving mad? This was an outrage! A disaster! He had been going to Pudsley Junior practically all his life! It was HIS school! He could walk there from his house, meeting Darren and Eugene on the way. He didn't want to go to some horrible new school where the teachers had you flogged for breathing too loud in class.

"Well I think it'll be nice," said Suzy.

"No it won't!" scowled Bertie. "It'll be horrible!"

"Just 'cos I'll have the biggest bedroom!" crowed Suzy.

"No you won't, smelly-pants!"

"Will!"

"Won't!"

"Stop squabbling!" cried Mum. "I'm sorry, Bertie, but Dad and I have decided and we're going. I'm sure once you've settled in you'll love it."

Bertie slumped back on the sofa and turned up the TV. It wasn't fair! Nobody asked if *he* wanted to move. Why were parents always ruining his life? Well they could move if they liked but he wasn't going. He would lock himself in his room and never come out. Ever.

…Except to order pizza.

FOR SALE:
Large house in
popular area.
Three beds.
Good size garden.
Nicer than it looks.

CHAPTER 2

A week passed and nothing more was said about the move. Bertie hoped Mum and Dad had forgotten the idea. But on Friday afternoon he was walking home from school with his friends when he spotted something in the window of Floggit's estate agents.

"That's MY house!" said Bertie.

Dirty Bertie

"Wow!" said Darren. "Looks like your mum and dad are really serious."

Bertie pressed his nose against the glass.

"This is terrible!" he said. "We've got to stop them!"

Darren shrugged. "What can we do?"

"Maybe no one will buy it," said Eugene, hopefully.

They walked on in gloomy silence. Bertie couldn't imagine living somewhere without his friends. If they moved he probably wouldn't *have* any friends.

"Couldn't you put them off?" said Eugene.

"Who?"

"The people buying your house. Tell them it's falling down or something."

Bertie shook his head. "They'll see it's not falling down."

"But Eugene's right," said Darren. "All you have to do is put them off!"

"How?" said Bertie.

"Easy! Tell them you've got vampires living next door."

"Tell them there's a body buried in the garden!"

"Tell them it's got fleas!"

"It's a house, not a dog!" said Bertie.

All the same, maybe Eugene had a point. He couldn't stop his parents selling the house, but maybe he could stop anyone from buying it! It would just take a few unpleasant surprises.

Dirty Bertie

Back home, Bertie got out his Top Secret Notebook and began to draw up his battle plan.

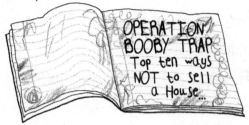

This was war.

Monday arrived. The first people to view the house were due at four and Mum was getting frantic.

"Bertie, have you tidied your room?"

"Yes!"

"And picked up your socks?"

"Yes!"

"And thrown away those rotten apple cores?"

Dirty Bertie

"Nearly!" shouted Bertie. Bertie had never seen his house looking so clean and tidy. Mum had swept and polished till it shone like a palace.

DING DONG!

Enemy attack. Bertie hurried downstairs. Operation Booby Trap was under way.

"Now remember," said Mum, "stay out of the way and don't touch anything. What's that you've got?"

"Where?"

"Behind your back."

Dirty Bertie

Bertie brought out a box. "Nothing. Just rubbish I'm throwing out."

"Hurry up then," said Mum, rushing to open the door.

"Mr and Mrs Mossop? Do come in! Shall we start in the lounge…?"

Battle stations! Bertie darted into the kitchen and closed the door. Setting the box down, he removed the lid and peeped inside.

"Time to come out!" he whispered.

Mum had finished showing the Mossops downstairs. Now for the bedrooms. She hoped Bertie had tidied his room.

"And this is my son's bedroom…" she said, opening the door.

Bertie looked up from
the book he was
pretending to read.
He was slightly
out of breath.

"Bertie, this is
Mr and Mrs
Mossop," said Mum.

"Pleased to meet you," smiled Bertie.

"What a nice quiet boy," said Mrs
Mossop. "And doesn't he keep his room
tidy?"

"Er … yes," said Mum, giving Bertie a
suspicious look. She closed the door.

Bertie listened as they went
downstairs. *Any second now*, he thought.

"ARGHHHHHHH!" Mrs Mossop
burst from the kitchen. "MICE!" she
shrieked. "You've got MICE!"

"I'm so sorry!" said Mum. "I can't think how they got there! Please don't go … maybe you'd like to see the garden?"

"No thank you!" bristled Mrs Mossop. "We've seen quite enough!"

The front door slammed. There was a heavy silence.

"BERTIE!" yelled Mum. "I want a word with you – NOW!"

Bertie crept downstairs. Mum was waiting for him with a face like thunder.

"All right, where did you get them?"

"Get what?" said Bertie.

"The mice. One of them ran up Mrs Mossop's leg!"

"Mice?" said Bertie, sounding amazed.

"I wasn't born yesterday, Bertie. The truth. *Where* did you get them?"

Bertie gulped. "Well … um …

I might've been looking after a couple of mice for Eugene. But I left them in their box."

Mum ground her teeth. "Listen to me," she said. "We are selling this house whether you like it or not. So you are not to bring mice, spiders, flies, beetles or any other creatures indoors. Do I make myself clear?"

"Yes," nodded Bertie. He tripped upstairs to his room and closed the door. Plan Number One had worked like a dream. It was a pity about spiders though because they were next on his list.

CHAPTER 3

The week passed. Visitors came and went. Mostly they went quickly as Bertie was lying in wait for them. He left taps running, muddy marks on walls and bars of soap where people could tread on them. Mum despaired. Dad threatened to stop his pocket money.

On Friday, Mum filled the dishwasher

and mopped the floor. No one had told her selling a house was so exhausting.

DING DONG! The Warners had arrived. Bertie was busy watching TV.

"Bertie, turn that off!" ordered Mum.

"But I'm watching *Alien Arthur*!"

"You can watch it later. And don't forget what I said – no more tricks!".

Mum rushed off to answer the door. Bertie heard voices in the hall and a small boy trooped into the lounge, followed by his mother.

"This is Mrs Warner and little George," said Mum.

George sucked his thumb and stared at Bertie.

Dirty Bertie

"Why don't we start in the back room," said Mum.

Bertie waited till they'd gone and sprang into action. Time for Brilliant Plan Number Eight.

Dashing to the kitchen, he filled Whiffer's bowl with doggy chunks and took it upstairs. Whiffer was dozing in his favourite spot on the landing. When he smelled the food he followed Bertie eagerly. Bertie opened the door of the airing cupboard.

"Good boy! In you go!" he whispered, placing the bowl inside. Whiffer jumped in and Bertie closed the door. Now for Phase Two. He took out Suzy's mobile and rang his home number. The phone downstairs began to ring. BLOOP! BLOOP! That should keep Mum busy for a while.

A moment later Mrs Warner popped her head round Bertie's door.

"Okay to look round?"

"Fine," said Bertie. "Did she warn you?"

"Sorry?" asked Mrs Warner.

"Oh, nothing!" Bertie went back to his book.

"Warn me about what?" Mrs Warner persisted.

"The house. You do know it's…" Bertie lowered his voice, "…*haunted?*"

Dirty Bertie

"HAUNTED?" Mrs Warner turned pale. George sucked his thumb. Bertie hit the REDIAL button on Suzy's phone.

"It's okay," said Bertie. "Usually he visits at night."

"Who?"

"The ghost!"

"Good heavens!" gasped Mrs Warner.

"It's my dog," Bertie explained. "He died last year, but now he's haunting us."

"You poor child!" Mrs Warner picked up George. "You've actually seen this ghost?"

"Oh yes!" said Bertie. "But mostly you hear him. You know, scratching and howling and so on. I expect you'll get used to it."

Mrs Warner looked worried. She didn't want to get used to it.

"Shhh!" Bertie held up a hand. "You hear that?"

They listened.

SCRATCH! SCRATCH! SCRATCH! Whiffer had finished his food and was pawing at the cupboard door.

"It's him – the ghost!" whispered Bertie. Mrs Warner held George tighter.

THUMP! THUMP!

"Oww oww owww!" whined Whiffer.

"That's it," gasped Mrs Warner. "We're leaving!"

They rushed downstairs and bumped into Mum in the hallway.

Dirty Bertie

"You're not going?" she said.

"We couldn't live here!" said Mrs Warner. "Not with that awful dog!"

"Oh. You mean Whiffer?" said Mum.

Mrs Warner looked at her. "You've seen him too?"

"Well of course!" laughed Mum. "I see him all the time. He lives here."

Mrs Warner stared at her in disbelief. "You're mad," she said, "mad!" and fled out the door.

Mum caught sight of Bertie watching over the banister. She narrowed her eyes.

"What was all that about?"

"Search me!" said Bertie. "I'll just … um … go and check on Whiffer."

CHAPTER 4

Sunday morning. Bertie was fixing himself
a snack. Dad was taking Suzy to her
dance lesson. Mum hoovered the hall,
dusted the mirror and tripped over
Bertie's shoes. She stuffed some roses
into a vase on the kitchen table.

"Flowers?" said Bertie.

"They make the house smell nice.

Dirty Bertie

We've got people coming."

"Not again!" moaned Bertie.

DING DONG! Dave and Debbie
Sweetly had arrived.

Mum took a deep breath. She wasn't
sure she could stand much more of this.
She hurried to the door.

"And Bertie," she said, "I'm warning
you … BEHAVE!"

Bertie thought quickly. So far
Operation Booby Trap had succeeded in
driving the enemy out. But he was
running out of ideas. How was he going
to get rid of these people? He stared
at the roses in the vase. Of course!
People wanted houses that smelled nice.
They didn't want houses that smelled
disgusting! What he needed was
something that really stank. Something

so pongy you would smell it through the whole house. Bertie looked out of the window. Whiffer was nosing in the flower beds. He squatted down behind a bush. That could only mean one thing... An idea began to take shape in Bertie's head. No, he couldn't. He daren't. On the other hand, this was war. He fetched the pooper scooper and hurried outside.

CREAK, CREAK!

Bertie sneaked up the stairs balancing a lump of dog poo on the pooper scooper. Now where to hide it? Somewhere for maximum stink effect. The bathroom? His mum and dad's bedroom? Of course – Suzy's room!

Downstairs he could hear the
Sweetlys talking in the lounge. He'd have
to move fast. Bertie opened Suzy's door
and slipped inside. His eye fell on her
jewellery box on top of the bookshelf.
No one would ever dream of looking
in there!

A minute later the Sweetlys came
upstairs.

"I love it, don't you, darling?" gushed
Debbie. "It's got tons of space and …
ohh!" She wrinkled her nose. "Can you
smell something?"

Dave sniffed. "Oh… Eugh! Yes I can."

"It smells like … well … um…"
Debbie turned to Mum. "Is your toilet
blocked?"

"I don't think so," said Mum. She sniffed. There *was* a nasty smell.

"Why don't I show you the main bedroom?" she said, quickly.

But Dave was heading for Suzy's room. "I think it's coming from here!" he said, opening the door.

The smell was overpowering. They reeled back, holding their noses.

"UGH! It stinks!" gasped Debbie.

"It's horrible!" moaned Dave. "Where's it coming from?"

"I've no idea!" said Mum. "It's my daughter's room. Normally it smells of nail varnish!"

Mum looked under the bed. Dave looked on the shelves. Debbie opened Suzy's jewellery box.

Inside was a ghastly brown blob.

"Oh! Ohhhhhh!" screamed Debbie.

"Come on, darling, we're going," said Dave, grimly.

THUD! The front door slammed.

Bertie waited in his room for Mum to shout his name. Silence. He crept slowly downstairs. Mum was in the kitchen, talking on the phone.

"Yes … I see… Well thanks for letting us know."

Dirty Bertie

"Who was that?" asked Bertie.

"The estate agent," said Mum, wearily.
"The house we wanted to buy has
been sold."

Bertie's face lit up. "Does that mean
we're not moving?"

Mum sighed heavily. "Okay. I give in.
I don't think I can take any more of
this."

Bertie danced round the kitchen. He'd
won! They were staying! Wait till he told
his friends!

Dirty Bertie

The front door banged. Suzy was back. She thumped upstairs.

Uh oh, thought Bertie. *I hope she doesn't go in…*

"ARGHHHHHHHHH!"